Sophie

McFall

Age 5

Sophies Book

This Treasury
belongs to

....

A Treasury
of Tales for
Bedtime

This is a Parragon book
This edition published in 2000

Parragon
Queen Street House
4 Queen Street
Bath BA1 1HE UK

Produced by
The Templar Company plc
Pippbrook Mill
London Road
Dorking, Surrey RH4 1JE UK

Printed and bound in Italy
ISBN 0 75253 473 4

A Treasury
of Tales for
Bedtime

p

Contents

PUFFCHEEK'S PALACE

"Pull!" cried Topknot, sitting on a grand
carriage he had found. The other elves
were pulling on a rope of woven grass,
towing his discovery into the woods.
Soon the pixies arrived to join in the fun.
"Push!" shouted Puffcheek to his fellow
pixies. So the elves pulled and the pixies
pushed, until the carriage wobbled and
Topknot almost fell off. "Pulling's safer
than pushing!" he called.
"But pushing's easier!" said Puffcheek,
and before Topknot could stop them, the
pixies gave a big shove. The carriage
shot forward so fast that the little elves
hardly had time to jump out of the way.

Topknot fell on the thick grass, and the carriage landed upside down in a ditch. "That was your fault, Puffcheek!" said Topknot crossly. "You pixies should be more careful!"

Just then, they heard loud voices approaching, and in a flash all the elves and pixies ran and hid. "There it is!" cried Kate, pointing. "What a place to leave your skateboard!"

"I didn't!" replied Sam. "I told you! I left it by a tree at the bottom of the garden. Someone must have moved it!"

"Pixies and elves, I suppose!" smiled Kate.

Sam laughed. He picked up his skateboard, then headed for home. Kate was about to follow when she saw the elves' grass rope that had broken free. Kate looked at it thoughtfully and put it in her pocket.

"So that's where the carriage came from," said Topknot, afterwards. "You mean skateboard," corrected Puffcheek.

"The Big People use all kinds of odd things and give them some very funny names!"
"Well, whatever they call it, I want it back!" cried Topknot. "Finders keepers!"
Even the pixies agreed, so Puffcheek promised to try and get it back.

When Puffcheek crept into
Kate's garden later that day,
she was sitting looking at the
little grass rope. Suddenly,
Kate sneezed and blew the
pixie backwards. "Hey! Look out!"
he yelled.
"Oh, there really are pixies," cried
Kate. "Did you make this rope!"
"No, it was the elves!" replied
Puffcheek, picking himself up.
"But I'll make you a grass bracelet
if you give me that carriage,
er, skateboard," he said.
"I was right! You did move it!"
said Kate. "But the
skateboard's not mine!"

Puffcheek explained what had happened. Then he sighed, "I can't return empty-handed to Topknot!" Kate had an idea. "Come back at sunset and I may be able to help!"

Kate went inside and found her brother.
"Could I have the toy castle you threw out
when you tidied your cupboard?" Kate
asked. Sam nodded. "I'm too big for it now!"
"I know someone who's just the right size!"
said Kate. At sunset, Puffcheek found
the little castle at the bottom
of the garden.
"I'm sorry I was cross with
you, Puffcheek!" said Topknot
as the elves and pixies
happily pushed and pulled
the toy castle deep into
the woods.

"A castle's better than a carriage any day!"
"You can call it 'Topknot's Castle',"
said Puffcheek.
"Or 'Puffcheek's Palace'," replied
Topknot kindly. "After all, you
were very brave to speak
to one of the Big People!"

Puffcheek smiled proudly as the elves and pixies congratulated him. Next morning, Sam followed his sister outside. "I saw you carrying my castle down to the bottom of the garden last night," he said.

"You wanted to play with it yourself, didn't you?"

"No, I left it here," replied Kate, pointing. "But it's gone!" "Just like my skateboard," said Sam. "Don't tell me you think the elves and pixies took my old toy castle too!"

Kate nodded. "Who else?" she smiled. "But this time, I think we'll let them keep it!"

THE LOST LAMB

One fine Spring day, Big Bear and his little
friend Morris Mouse were going for a walk
in the countryside. But they had not gone
very far when they met a little lamb who was
lost. The lamb explained that the farmer had
been moving all the sheep to a different
field. She had stopped to munch on some nice
white flowers, and when she looked up
everyone had disappeared. "If only I hadn't
been so greedy!" she bleated.
"Don't worry," said Big Bear kindly.
"I understand. My stomach is always getting
me into trouble too! We'll help you find
your friends."

So they set off in search of Lamb's friends,
but although they looked far and wide
there was no sign of them anywhere.
"We've been walking for hours,"
said Big Bear. "All the fields seem
to look the same ."
"I think we've been walking
in circles," said Morris.
"Do you think we're lost too?"

"We may have lost our way, but I haven't lost my appetite," groaned Big Bear. "I wish we'd brought a picnic!" They had just stopped to ask a passing goose for help, when Olive Owl came by. "I'm sure I heard some sheep in that field over there," she said, pointing up a big hill.

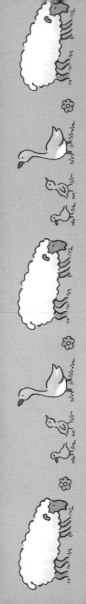

Big Bear puffed and panted as they climbed the big hill. "I hope this isn't a wild goose chase!" he joked. But when they got to the field all they found was Gertie Goat.

"I suppose goats do sound a bit like sheep," said Morris.

The little lamb started to cry. "I'm never going to find my friends," she sobbed. Big Bear bent to stroke her, and she was crying so loudly he didn't hear the thundering hooves behind him until it was too late.

"Look out, Big Bear!" cried Morris.

BAM!

With a toss of his horns Bertie Bull sent
Big Bear flying through the air. He sailed
over the hedge and landed in a crumpled
heap in something soft and white
and woolly...

Percy Pig the farmer had been shearing the
sheep, and Big Bear had landed right in the
pile of sheepskins! Morris and the little lamb
came hurrying along close behind him.
"Hooray," cried the lamb.
"You've found my
friends!" Big Bear
brushed himself
off and smiled.
"For a minute
there I thought
I'd squashed them!"
he said, and everyone
laughed. The farmer thanked
Big Bear, and invited them to
the farmhouse for tea.
Big Bear's stomach
rumbled.
"If you insist," he
said. "I think I
could manage a
bite or two!"

The Tooth Fairy

One day, Thomas went to tea at Grandma's. Everything was delicious — except for the rock cakes, which were like — um — rocks. As he bit into one his wobbly tooth came out. "Lucky Thomas!" said Grandma. "Take it home and put it under your pillow for the Tooth Fairy!"

Grandma went into the kitchen, and Thomas hid the rest of his cake in her droopy pot plant, as usual.

That night Thomas put his tooth under his pillow and went to sleep. The next morning, his tooth had gone — and there was a shiny new coin instead! Thomas was very pleased. Now he had nearly enough money to buy a new football!

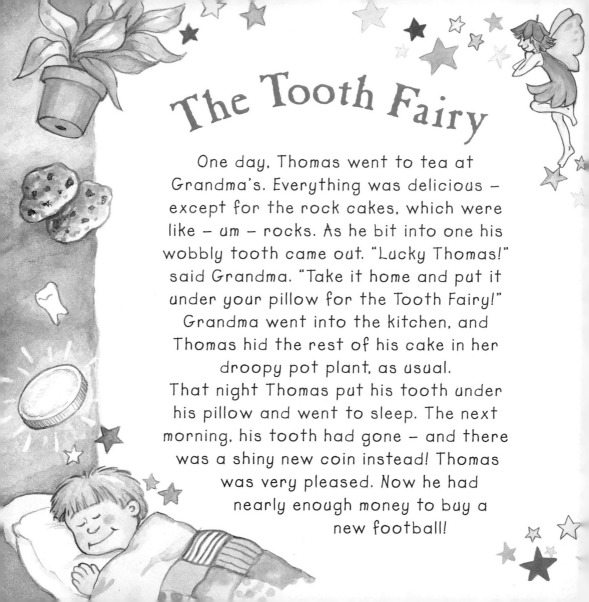

The next week, Thomas found another wobbly tooth. He wiggled and jiggled it, but it wouldn't budge, so he went to see Grandma again. He bravely bit into one of her rock cakes, and out came the tooth! Thomas really wanted to know what the Tooth Fairy was going to do with his tooth So that night, he left a note on his pillow: "Dear Tooth Fairy, I have a tooth for you. If you wake me up you can have it. Love, Thomas." Later that night he woke to see a fairy creature on his pillow, "Hello," said Thomas. "If you don't mind me asking, why do you want my tooth?"

The Tooth Fairy smiled. "Come with me," she said, pointing a tiny remote control at Thomas ... "WOW!" – Thomas was standing in a huge room that sparkled and shone. In the middle of the room was a big machine. At one end a bucketful of teeth was being poured into a funnel. From the other came a fine, sparkly powder. It fell onto a conveyor belt, and was dropped into little sacks. Hundreds of fairies were busy everywhere.

"Your tooth will go into the funnel," said the Tooth Fairy. "We use children's teeth to make fairy dust. It's the secret ingredient in lots of our spells. Teeth are very valuable to us fairies. That's why we always pay you."
Thomas gazed in amazement.
"I have to take tonight's teeth to the stores," said the Fairy, "But since you're here, I'll grant you three wishes." Thomas could hardly believe his luck! He closed his eyes and took a deep breath.
"I wish that I could buy my new football ... I wish that Grandma's rock cakes were light and fluffy ... and I wish that her pot plant would get better..."

Before he could finish speaking, the fairy factory had vanished, and he was back in bed, holding a shiny coin. He emptied his piggy bank — now there was enough for the new football! He took it to Grandma's the next week when he went for tea.

"Very nice, dear," said Grandma, as she brought in some rock cakes fresh from the oven. Thomas took a big bite. It was soft and crumbly, and full of big, juicy currants.

"These are great, Grandma!" he said.

"You tuck in while I water my pot plant," said Grandma. "It's coming on a treat."

A SEASIDE ADVENTURE

The sun beat down on Dotty Dog,
as she lay relaxing on the beach, listening
to the gentle lapping of the waves.
"Ahh, this is the life," she thought to herself.
"Peace and quiet. No postmen to chase. No
intruders to watch out for. Nothing
to worry about..."
Her friends, Billy Bear and Rosy Rabbit had
been busy building a sandcastle. "We're going
for a swim to cool down, Dotty," said Rosy.
"Do you want to come?"
"No, thank you," said Dotty. "I think I'll just
lay here and enjoy the peace!"

Dotty lay dozing in the sun. She could hear their excited shouts, as Billy and Rosy played in the waves. Before long she fell fast asleep and began to dream...

The waves lapped against the sides of her boat as she scanned the horizon through her telescope. She was the captain of a pirate ship, and Rosy and Billy were her faithfull crew. They had discovered treasure and now the fearsome Pirate King was after them. Now they had to reach safety before the Bearded Pirate could catch them!

Just then a thick mist came down, blocking their view. And out of nowhere a huge dark shape appeared, looming through the mist. It was the Bearded Pirate's great boat, drawing up alongside them! Billy and Rosy leapt into the water with a loud splash. Dotty was about to follow, but The Pirate King had caught her by the tail -
"Look out Dotty!" cried Billy.

Dotty woke with a start and leapt to her
feet. A large crab was holding her tail firmly
in it's pincers. "Ouch!" From the beach she
could hear Billy calling "Look out!"
Dotty soon shook off the crab.
"Thank goodness for that," she said with
relief. "I thought I'd been caught by The
Pirate King" She told the others about her
dream and everyone laughed.
Soon they were packed up and
ready to leave.
"It will be nice to get home for some peace
and quiet," said Dotty. "After all,
postmen are much easier to deal with
than pirates!"

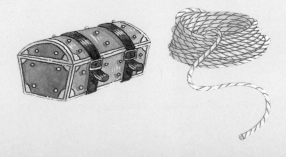

Grandma

Ma & Pa Jam

Big Bamboo

Jim Jam

Peaches & Plum

Grandma

Ma & Pa Jam

Big Bamboo

Meet the Jam Pandas

One sunny day the Jam Pandas arrived at
Tumbledown Cottage in a big truck. They
had been left the cottage and orchard
by their Great Uncle Greengage. He had
spent all of his time in the orchard, and
the cottage was in a mess.
"Never mind," said Grandma cheerfully.
"We'll soon clean it up."
"Come along, everybody," said Pa.
"Let's unload the truck."

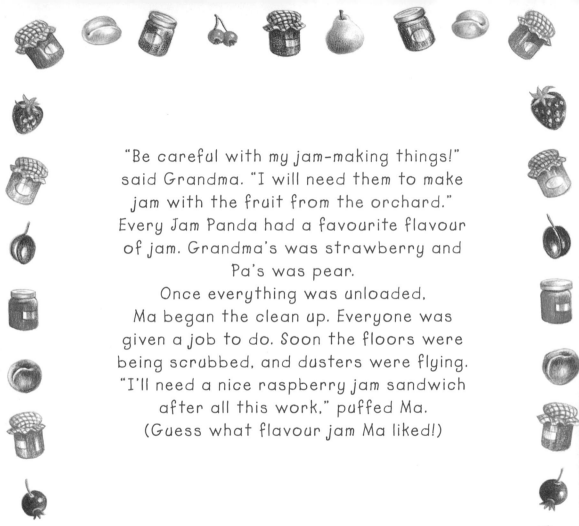

"Be careful with my jam-making things!"
said Grandma. "I will need them to make
jam with the fruit from the orchard."
Every Jam Panda had a favourite flavour
of jam. Grandma's was strawberry and
Pa's was pear.
Once everything was unloaded,
Ma began the clean up. Everyone was
given a job to do. Soon the floors were
being scrubbed, and dusters were flying.
"I'll need a nice raspberry jam sandwich
after all this work," puffed Ma.
(Guess what flavour jam Ma liked!)

Grandma

Ma & Pa Jam

Big Bamboo

Jim Jam

Peaches & Plum

Grandma

Ma & Pa Jam

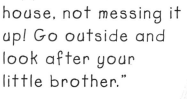
Big Bamboo

Peaches and Plum went to explore the rest of the house. The old rooms were dark and dusty – just right for hiding and jumping out on poor Grandma! The naughty twins were always playing tricks. They chased each other up the stairs. "Look at me!" cried Peaches, jumping on an old bed. Soon Peaches and Plum were fighting with the pillows. Feathers were flying everywhere.

"Jumping Jamspoons!" cried Ma, coming into the room. "We're supposed to be cleaning the house, not messing it up! Go outside and look after your little brother."

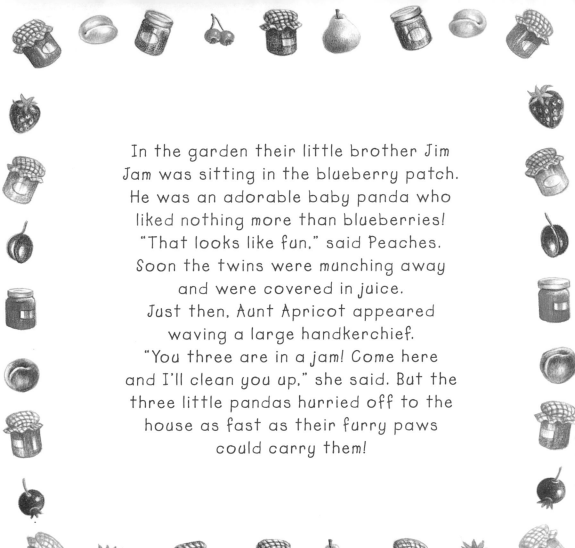

In the garden their little brother Jim
Jam was sitting in the blueberry patch.
He was an adorable baby panda who
liked nothing more than blueberries!
"That looks like fun," said Peaches.
Soon the twins were munching away
and were covered in juice.
Just then, Aunt Apricot appeared
waving a large handkerchief.
"You three are in a jam! Come here
and I'll clean you up," she said. But the
three little pandas hurried off to the
house as fast as their furry paws
could carry them!

Grandma

Ma & Pa Jam

Big Bamboo

Jim Jam

Peaches & Plum

Grandma

Ma & Pa Jam

Big Bamboo

Back in the kitchen Big Bamboo, the eldest son, was busy. He blushed pink when the others appeared. "What are you up to now?" asked Ma, with a sigh. "Just testing the jam in case it went bad on the journey," said Big Bamboo, who was very greedy. "Well I think it's time for tea," said Ma. And so the Jam Pandas settled down to the first of many jammy teatimes in their new home . "I think we're going to be happy here," said Grandma, and everyone agreed.

The Jam Panda Picnic

One Spring day Peaches and Plum woke
up early and hurried downstairs. They
were excited, because today the Jam
Pandas were having a picnic in Bluebell
Wood. They helped Grandma pack the
picnic basket full of lovely things to eat.
There were sandwiches spread with
delicious jams. There were jam tarts,
jam sponges and best of all,
jam doughnuts!

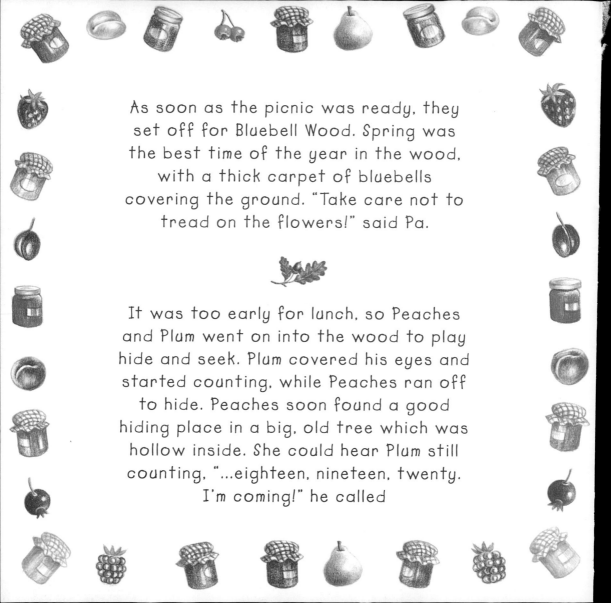

As soon as the picnic was ready, they set off for Bluebell Wood. Spring was the best time of the year in the wood, with a thick carpet of bluebells covering the ground. "Take care not to tread on the flowers!" said Pa.

It was too early for lunch, so Peaches and Plum went on into the wood to play hide and seek. Plum covered his eyes and started counting, while Peaches ran off to hide. Peaches soon found a good hiding place in a big, old tree which was hollow inside. She could hear Plum still counting, "...eighteen, nineteen, twenty. I'm coming!" he called

Peaches didn't think it would take Plum long to find her. She waited and waited. But Plum didn't come. After a while, she called out, "Plum, I'm here!" But Plum still didn't come. Peaches decided that she had waited long enough. She didn't want to miss lunch! She crawled out of her hiding place and set off back to the picnic. But poor Peaches couldn't find her way back! She walked on and on through Bluebell Wood. "Ma!" she cried. "Pa! Grandma!" But no-one answered. Peaches was lost. She sat down on a tree stump and started to cry.

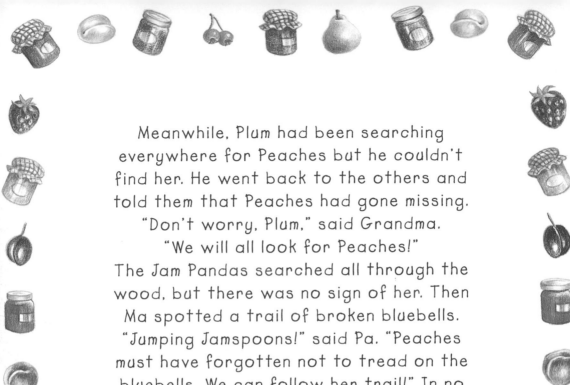

Meanwhile, Plum had been searching
everywhere for Peaches but he couldn't
find her. He went back to the others and
told them that Peaches had gone missing.
"Don't worry, Plum," said Grandma.
"We will all look for Peaches!"
The Jam Pandas searched all through the
wood, but there was no sign of her. Then
Ma spotted a trail of broken bluebells.
"Jumping Jamspoons!" said Pa. "Peaches
must have forgotten not to tread on the
bluebells. We can follow her trail!" In no
time at all, the trail led the Jam Pandas to
Peaches. She was fast asleep under a
tree. Plum woke her up with a big hug.
They were very glad to see each other!

Just then, Big Bamboo's tummy rumbled and everyone laughed. "I think it's picnic time," said Grandma. Back at the picnic spot they were soon tucking into a delicious jammy feast. Ma made sure Peaches got a specially big helping of her favourite peach jam.
"At least one thing is certain," chuckled Pa, biting into a big jammy doughnut. "When it comes to picnics, Grandma always makes sure nothing is missing!"

Wash Day Blues

Wishy Washy lived above his shop, 'Wishy's Washeteria', in fairyland. He spent each day hand-washing fairy wings, which was a very important job.

This week he was busier than ever. There was going to be a big party on Saturday. The fairy council would choose which lucky fairies would sit on top of the Christmas trees this year.

All the fairies needed their wings washed by Saturday, as they wanted to look their best.

"I'll never be finished in time," Wishy said to himself. "I'll have to buy a washing machine." He phoned and ordered one, and it was delivered right away.

His new
machine was
very big and covered
in buttons and
flashing lights. Wishy
started to read the
instructions, but they were
very complicated so he filled
the machine and put it on what he
thought was a low setting. Then
he hurried out to the final of the
fairyland quiz competition. He
wanted to win the prize money so
that he could go on holiday, as he
had not been away for years. To his
surprise, Wishy won the competition
and a thousand fairy pieces!
He could not believe his luck.
A lovely new washing
machine and winning
the competition all
in one day!

He went home and straight to bed, tired but happy. But as he lay in bed he thought he heard a rumbling noise below. He went downstairs to the laundry, and could not believe his eyes!

The floor was covered in soap suds, which were pouring out of his new machine. He ran to turn it off.

"Oh no, what a mess!" he said. He pulled the wings out of the machine, but every single pair was ruined. Some had stretched, some had shrunk, and others were full of holes! Wishy sat down and cried. "All the wings are ruined and the fairies need them for Saturday. What am I going to do?"

Wishy spent all night clearing up the soapy mess. "This will teach me not to be impatient. If only I'd washed them by hand!" he said to himself. Next day, Wishy explained what had happened to the fairies. Using his prize money, he gave each of them enough to buy a new pair of wings. By the end of the day he only had twenty fairy pieces left.

"I can always go on holiday next year," sighed Wishy.

On Saturday night the fairies gathered to hear who had been chosen to decorate the Christmas trees. They looked lovely with their shiny new wings.

By now, everyone knew what had happened to Wishy, and that he had spent his prize money on the new wings. There was a special announcement.

"You are a hard working, kind and honest fairy, Wishy Washy," said the Fairy Speaker. "Your friends and customers have collected some money for you. Everyone thinks you deserve a holiday. Enjoy your trip!"

Wishy thanked everyone, and thought how lucky he was to have his little shop, such caring friends, and a lovely holiday to look forward to.

CRASH LANDING!

"Come along, Big Bear," said Morris Mouse,
jumping up and down with excitement. "Let's
go for a cycle ride. Exercise helps to keep
you fit and healthy, you know."
"Only if we can take a picnic," said Big Bear.
"A big bear like me needs to refuel every so
often." So they packed up a picnic and set
off. "Have a nice day!" waved Olive Owl.

"Which way shall we go, Big Bear?" asked Morris, as they came to a crossroads. "Let's head out into the countryside," said Big Bear. "It's quiet and peaceful there, away from all the dangerous traffic in town." The two friends cycled happily along looking at all the trees and animals that they passed on their way. After a while, they stopped in a shady spot beneath a big oak tree to eat their picnic. "This is the life!" said Big Bear as he lay back for a quick snooze after lunch.

Soon they were back on the road again. "I've got much more energy after some food and a nap," Big Bear called to Morris. "See how fast I can cycle now!" and he whizzed on ahead as fast as he could. "Wait for me!" called Morris, as he struggled to keep up. Just then, a small aeroplane zoomed overhead, flying loop the loops. "I wish I could do that," thought Big Bear. He was so busy speeding along and watching the plane, that he didn't see the tractor in the road ahead of him. "Look out, Big Bear!" called Morris Mouse. But he was too far behind for Big Bear to hear him.

Big Bear's cycle hit the tractor, and he went
flying through the air in a loop the loop,
before landing with a crash on his bottom!
"Thank goodness I have lots of padding!"
said Big Bear. Puffing and panting,
Morris Mouse arrived.
"Are you alright, Big Bear?" he asked in
a worried voice.
"Just a few bangs and scrapes," said Big Bear.
"So much for avoiding the dangerous traffic
in town!" said Morris.
"And so much for exercise keeping you fit and
healthy!" said Big Bear. "From now on let's
just stick to picnics!"

THE FORGETFUL BEAR

Belinda Bear was such a forgetful
bear. Nearly everyone forgets a
friend's birthday at some time in their lives,
but this year the birthday that Belinda had
forgotten was her own! Imagine forgetting
your own birthday! Just the night before,
Mummy had tucked her into bed, and asked,
"Are you looking forward to tomorrow?"
"Of course," said Belinda. "It's Saturday.
I love Saturdays!" Mummy smiled.
"Aren't you forgetting something?" asked
Daddy. Belinda thought hard. "Ooh, yes. We're
having pancakes for breakfast. Yummy!"

The next morning Belinda laid in bed snoring, while the rest of the family were busy getting ready for her birthday. She had forgotten all about the pancakes.

By the time she came downstairs, everything was ready for her party.

But when she saw the balloons in the hallway, Belinda felt very worried indeed. It must be someone's birthday – but whose? Whoever it was, she had forgotten to buy them a present. What was she going to do?

All the family were waiting as she stepped into the living room. "Surprise!" they called. "Happy Birthday, Belinda!" Belinda blushed from head to paw.

"Silly me," she said. "The birthday I've forgotten is my own! At least I didn't need to buy a present."

"But we did," said Mummy, and they each handed her a gift. Belinda was delighted to have so many unexpected gifts, including a lovely new party dress from Mummy.

"Hurry up and put it on," said Mummy. "Your party will start soon!"

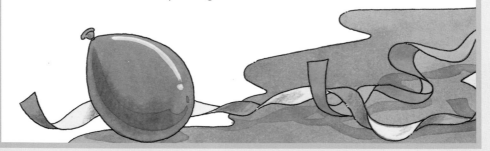

Belinda's friends began arriving soon afterwards, and each of them brought her a present. They played all sorts of party games, then sat down to eat the wonderful tea that Mummy had made for them. They could hardly believe it when they heard that Belinda had forgotten her own birthday. "You'll forget your own name next!" they teased. Just then, Mummy appeared carrying a large birthday cake.

"How old are you, Belinda?" asked Sam Squirrel. Belinda thought a moment.

"I'm five," she said. "I thought you were going to say you'd forgotten," said Sam. "Well, I was," blushed Belinda. "But then I counted the candles on my cake!" and everyone laughed.

Grandma's Strawberry Surprise

Grandma was very proud of the lovely
jams she made, especially the strawberry
jam, which was her favourite. But one day,
when Grandma went to get some
strawberry jam from the cupboard for
tea, she got a shock. It was all gone –
Big Bamboo had eaten the very last jar!
"Oh well," said Grandma. "I will make some
more." But the strawberries had not been
growing well that year. They didn't
look big enough to make jam with.
Then Grandma had an idea...

In the kitchen, Grandma got out her
special book. It was very old. It had
been given to her by her Great-Grandma.
She searched through the dusty pages
until she found the recipe for a magic
growing potion. Grandma
was going to make some
to put on the little
strawberries
in the garden.
Soon Grandma was
busy preparing the
magic potion.
She didn't
notice that
Big Bamboo
had eaten one
of the secret
ingredients while
she wasn't looking.

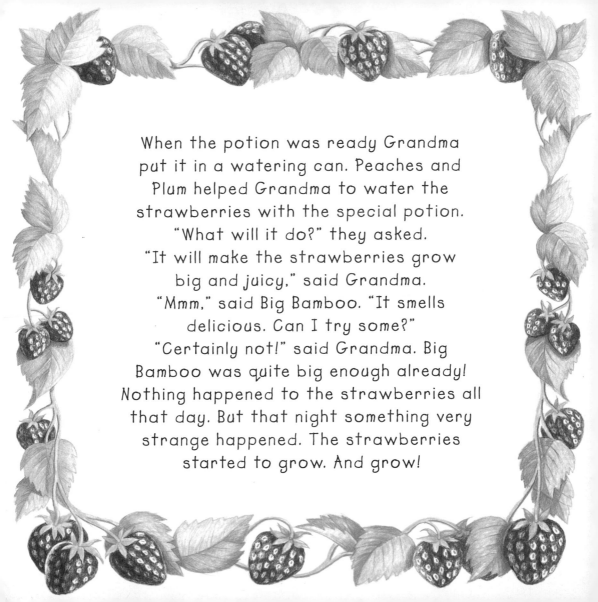

When the potion was ready Grandma
put it in a watering can. Peaches and
Plum helped Grandma to water the
strawberries with the special potion.
"What will it do?" they asked.
"It will make the strawberries grow
big and juicy," said Grandma.
"Mmm," said Big Bamboo. "It smells
delicious. Can I try some?"
"Certainly not!" said Grandma. Big
Bamboo was quite big enough already!
Nothing happened to the strawberries all
that day. But that night something very
strange happened. The strawberries
started to grow. And grow!

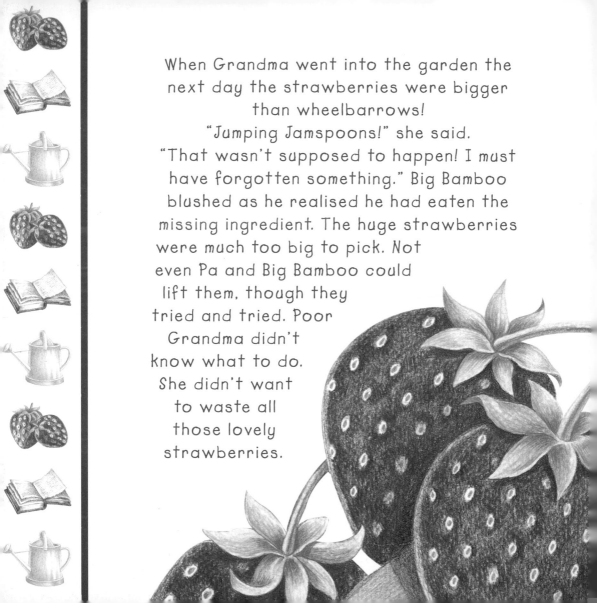

When Grandma went into the garden the next day the strawberries were bigger than wheelbarrows!

"Jumping Jamspoons!" she said. "That wasn't supposed to happen! I must have forgotten something." Big Bamboo blushed as he realised he had eaten the missing ingredient. The huge strawberries were much too big to pick. Not even Pa and Big Bamboo could lift them, though they tried and tried. Poor Grandma didn't know what to do. She didn't want to waste all those lovely strawberries.

Then she had
another idea.
She told Peaches
and Plum that she
had a special job
for them to do...

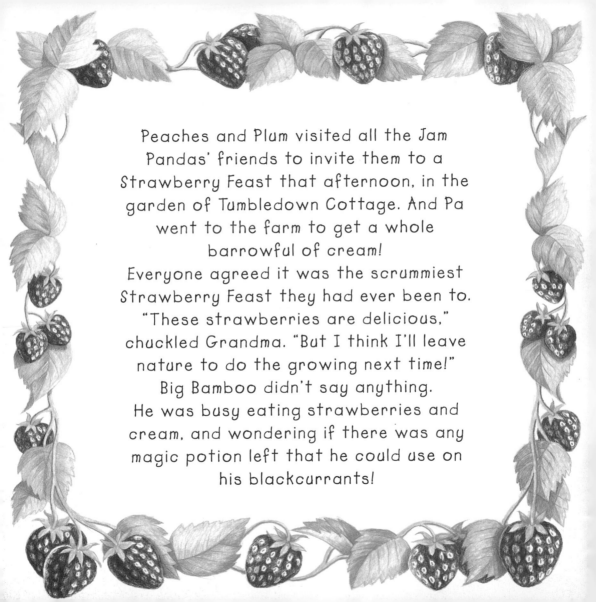

Peaches and Plum visited all the Jam Pandas' friends to invite them to a Strawberry Feast that afternoon, in the garden of Tumbledown Cottage. And Pa went to the farm to get a whole barrowful of cream!

Everyone agreed it was the scrummiest Strawberry Feast they had ever been to. "These strawberries are delicious," chuckled Grandma. "But I think I'll leave nature to do the growing next time!"

Big Bamboo didn't say anything. He was busy eating strawberries and cream, and wondering if there was any magic potion left that he could use on his blackcurrants!

THE BUSY DAY

Big Bear was a very kind bear, who always tried to help others when they had a problem. Which is why Olive Owl the schoolteacher had asked him for his help today. The school children had been practising letter-writing, and they had been looking forward to the postman collecting the letters they had written. But the postman had been taken ill.

"I'd be delighted to deliver the letters," said Big Bear.

"All that walking will be good exercise."

"And exercise is just what you need, after eating all those cream buns for breakfast!" said his friend Morris Mouse.

Morris Mouse decided to go along and help. Big Bear put the big heavy sack of letters on his shoulder and they set off. There seemed to be letters for everyone. All day long they walked around the town, delivering letters to the butcher, the baker, the doctor, the milkman and even the bus driver - although Big Bear had to chase the bus all the way down the high street before he could catch it! The bus took them out into the countryside, where they found Percy Pig, the farmer, busy with his tractor. "Thanks for coming all this way," he said, and put the letter in his pocket.

By the end of the day, Big Bear was exhausted. He sank down beneath a tree and sighed. "Thank goodness we've finished. I haven't got the energy to deliver one more letter!" he said.

"Well, it's a good job I have," said Morris Mouse, taking the last letter out of the sack. "Because this last letter is addressed to you!" Big Bear felt quite excited. He hadn't had a letter for years.

"Open it up, Morris. What does it say?" he asked. Morris ripped it open.

Inside was an invitation for them both to attend a tea party with the children at the school that afternoon.

When they got there they found everyone
else they had delivered a letter to, having a
party with the children. Everyone
cheered when they arrived.
"We would have missed the
party if you and Morris
hadn't delivered the letters,
Big Bear," said Freddie Fox.
"No problem!" said Big Bear.
"But all that walking has
given me quite an appetite!"
and he took a bite of
a big cream bun.
"Looks like we're back
where we started!"
sighed Morris. "But if
you can't beat them,
join them!" and he
munched happily on jam
tarts until it was time
to go home!

Ozzie Flies His Kite

"Follow me!" cried Ozzie Ostrich, as he ran ahead of his friends. It was a fine, blustery day and they were heading for the park. "Slow down, Ozzie. Wait for me!" called Billy Bear, who was puffing and panting, trying to keep up with the rest of the group. "Certainly not!" replied Ozzie. "These legs were built for speed. Just what I need to fly my new kite. I'm not waiting for a slow coach like you!" And he raced on ahead.

Billy Bear sat down on the pavement to catch his breath. He knew Ozzie was excited about his new kite, but he wished he hadn't been so mean.

"I thought Ozzie was my friend," Billy said miserably. "Friends should look after each other."

"Cheer up," said Freddie Fox, who was waiting for him. "I'm a bit of a slow coach too!"

By the time they got to the park, the others were busy having fun. Ozzie whizzed past with his new kite flying high in the sky behind him. "Look at me!" he called.

For a long time Ozzie raced up and down with his new kite, while the others played happily on the swings and slides.

"Can I have a go with your kite, Ozzie?" asked Billy. "Don't be silly," scoffed Ozzie. "A slow little bear like you couldn't fly a kite. You can't run fast enough!" And on he ran, faster and faster, and his kite flew higher and higher. "Look how clever I am," he called. "I can make my kite fly as high as the trees!"

But Ozzie was running so fast that he didn't see the great oak tree until it was too late! His kite hit the tree and got stuck high up in the branches! "Oh, no!" sobbed Ozzie. "My beautiful kite! What am I going to do? I'll never reach it up there." The others came running over at once.

"Don't cry, Ozzie," said Billy Bear. "I'll soon get it down for you."

In no time at all, Billy climbed the tree using his sharp claws to cling to the bark, and rescued the kite.

"Oh, thank you, Billy," said Ozzie, looking ashamed. "You are kind to help me after I was so nasty and rude to you. I'm really very sorry."
"It's okay," said Billy. "That's what friends are for."
Just then it started to rain. "We'd better race for home," cried Dotty Dog, "before we get soaked!" And off the friends ran through the rain. But this time Ozzie made sure he ran at the very back and waited for his good friend Billy.

The Bottom of the Garden

Did you know there might be fairies living at the bottom of your garden? There was once an old house that had been empty for years. The garden was as wild as a jungle. The grass was so high it tickled your knees, and it was tangled with wild flowers. It looked a mess, but it was full of life – butterflies, birds, mice and hedgehogs all made their homes there. And the garden was the home of some other little creatures, too. Until, that is, the new owners moved in.

One morning, Lucy and her parents arrived
in a big van. The grown-ups unloaded the
van, while Lucy went to explore. Dad had
promised her a swing for the garden.
But she was amazed when she saw how
overgrown the garden was. She sat down
and tried to imagine it all tidied up with
her swing in the corner.
"Excuse me," said a tiny voice. Lucy looked
around. "I'm up here," said the little voice.
Lucy rubbed her eyes. A tiny person
with flower petals on her head
was sitting on the bird table.
She looked just like a fairy in
one of Lucy's books.

"Are you moving in?"
asked the fairy.
"Because this is our
garden and we don't
want it spoiled by people
with big boots and spades and
lawnmowers and weedkillers..."
Before Lucy could answer,
Dad came into the garden.
"I'm going to clear the whole garden
and lay a new lawn," he said.
"Your swing could go in that corner."
With that he went back into the house.
"This is terrible," said the fairy.
"This garden has been our home for
years. We'll all have to find somewhere
else to live." As Lucy listened, dozens
of little fairies appeared.

"Can you help us?" asked one.
"The other gardens are too tidy around
here. Where will we go?" said another.
Lucy's mother called to her from the house.
"I promise I'll think of something to
help you, " said Lucy, as she got
up and went inside.
A week later a new garden shed and
a shiny set of gardening tools
were delivered.
"I can't wait to start on this garden!"
said Dad rubbing his hands
together. "You'll soon have your
swing up, Lucy!"
Lucy felt terrible. She still
hadn't thought of a plan to
save the fairies!

If she didn't think of something soon,
they'd be homeless!

She sat in her bedroom, gazing out at the garden and watching a fairy collecting cobwebs outside her window. A butterfly fluttered by and settled on the window ledge. "I've got it!" cried Lucy suddenly. "I know just what to do!"
That evening, Lucy ate her tea with her mum and dad. "Dad," she said, "I've had a lovely idea for the garden."

"Don't talk to me about the garden,"
said Dad, gloomily. "It's going to take me
forever to tidy it. It took me all day just
to clear a corner for the shed."
"Then why don't we leave the bottom half
as a wildlife garden?" said Lucy. "Then
all the butterflies and birds and—er—other
little creatures — will still have a home!"
Dad cheered up
immediately. Only half
the work to do!
So that's what they did.
Dad made a pond in the wildlife
garden. Lucy sat on her swing
and smiled as she watched
the fairies playing on the pond.
She had kept her promise.

Big Bamboo's Blackcurrant Birthday

Big Bamboo was such a lazy panda. One morning he woke up very late. As he lay dozing he heard strange noises coming from downstairs. What was all that banging and clattering? "Oh, no!" said Big Bamboo. "Work!"
Big Bamboo didn't like work. He climbed out of bed and got dressed. Then he crept downstairs and sneaked out of the house. He was going to find somewhere to hide so he wouldn't have to work! He didn't realise the other Jam Pandas had heard him. They were looking at each other, smiling.

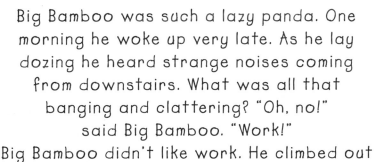

Big Bamboo didn't know that the 'work' was all for him! He wasn't very good at remembering things and had forgotten that today was his birthday. The other Jam Pandas were busy preparing a special birthday party for him.

At last everything was ready. The cottage was decorated with balloons, and the table was covered with jam sandwiches, jam sponges and even jam jelly! There were party hats and a lot of presents. All they needed now was Big Bamboo and the party could begin. But where was he?

The Jam Pandas set out to look for him.
First they looked in the garden.
"He can't be far away," said Ma Jam.
But he wasn't in the garden.
"Perhaps he's in the orchard," said Grandma.
But he wasn't in the orchard.
"Maybe he's in the wood," said Pa. But Big
Bamboo wasn't there either. Just then
little Jim Jam, the baby panda, began
crawling away. "Big Bam! Big Bam!" he said.
"Jumping Jamspoons!" said Grandma.
"That little chap's got an idea!"
Jim Jam was heading for the blackcurrant
patch. Peaches and Plum were close behind
him. "Look!" they shouted, pointing at the
blackcurrant patch. "It's Big Bamboo!"

Big Bamboo loved blackcurrants. They were his very favourite fruit. He had been hiding there all morning and had eaten nearly every blackcurrant in the patch! Now he looked like a very poorly panda indeed. "Ooooh!" he groaned. "My tummy hurts!" Back at the cottage, Big Bamboo went straight to bed. Grandma made a pot of special medicinal jam. Before long, Big Bamboo was feeling better, but he was very disappointed that he had missed his party, and spoiled his big surprise. "I'm very sorry," he told the others. "I'll try not to be so greedy in future."

The next day he got up, went
downstairs and... Surprise!

HAPPY BIRTHDAY
BIG BAMBOO!

The Jam Pandas had decided that Big
Bamboo had suffered enough for his
greediness, and to hold the party a day
late. Besides, it would be terrible to
waste all those lovely jam sandwiches!